Tales of
KING ARTHUR

Tales of
KING ARTHUR

RETOLD BY DANIEL RANDALL AND RONNE RANDALL
ILLUSTRATED BY GRAHAM HOWELLS

BARNES & NOBLE

NEW YORK

This 2004 edition published by Barnes & Noble, Inc.,
by arrangement with Bookmart Ltd.

ISBN 13: 978-0-7607-5259-3
ISBN 10: 0-7607-5259-1

Printed and bound in Thailand

3 5 7 9 10 8 6 4 2

CONTENTS

INTRODUCTION

The legends of King Arthur are among the richest and most mysterious in British folklore. Besides being exciting stories, they deal with important and timeless themes such as justice and the struggle for power.

There almost certainly was a real leader named Arthur, but he was probably not High King of all Britain. The Celtic people were still living in clans, and the rivalries between these clans were so deep that it was unlikely they would have chosen one king to rule over them all. In his legendary role as Pendragon, Arthur represents the ideal of unity, something many Celts may have wanted, but never really achieved.

The hero we know as King Arthur was probably a clan chieftain who most likely came from Cornwall, Wales, or Scotland, and lived between AD 450 and 530,

not long after the end of Roman rule in Britain. He used tactical and military skills learned from the Romans to ward off Saxon invaders. His most important recorded victory was at Mount Badon, where one account says he killed 926 men single-handedly. This probably isn't accurate, but it tells us that he was a skilled and much-admired warrior.

Tales of Arthur's deeds spread throughout Britain, and in the 1100s the bishop Geoffrey of Monmouth recorded his version of the Arthur legends in his book *The History of the Kings of Britain.* The stories spread across the sea to France, where, in the twelfth and thirteenth centuries, poets like Chrétien de Troyes added to the legends by introducing romantic characters, such as Lancelot.

Since then, countless poets, historians, playwrights, and, more recently, filmmakers have added their own versions of the Arthurian legend. It can be difficult to find one's way through all these stories to the true Arthur at their heart. But one thing is not difficult to find—the richness of the legends, and of the messages they carry. The stories of this fiery Celtic warrior echo through the ages, making him a hero for all time.

PROLOGUE

When the Romans came to Britain, Rome was a mighty empire, whose rule extended over much of the known world. Britain, an island standing alone in northwestern Europe, was to be its final northern frontier. The land was green and fertile, with valuable resources to be mined in its hills. Emperor Claudius conquered the island in AD 43, and Britain remained part of Rome for more than three hundred years.

But with time, the might of the Roman Empire crumbled, and it began losing territories. Britain was one of them. Menaced by native tribes and by Saxons across the sea, the Romans knew their time in Britain was coming to an end. Gradually, they began sailing for home, leaving Britain in chaos.

The native peoples of Britain fought with each other. Those who had taken up Christianity, the new

religion of Rome, warred against those who had stayed true to the Celtic religion. Tribes from the north made raiding trips south, and Saxon tribes from across the sea were a constant threat.

A land that had once flourished was being torn apart. It had been plunged into darkness, and few could see the light.

But out of the darkness came hope, in the form of a great man, a man who would heal the rifts that had split his country, and unite his people. He would drive the invaders back, and make Britain whole again.

The story of this extraordinary man and his deeds lived on long after he was gone, and spread throughout the world. It is the story of King Arthur, and there is magic in its telling.

UTHER AND IGRAINE

It was a troubled time for the island of Britain. The Romans had left, and now the Celts battled viciously among themselves. Britain and her people were being destroyed.

A warrior named Uther showed great bravery and skill in these wars, and he soon rose to become Pendragon, High King of all Britain. He knew that his first task must be to unite his kingdom by getting the warring chieftains to join together under his leadership.

Uther Pendragon could be hot-tempered and thoughtless, so he asked his most trusted advisor, Merlin, to help him. Merlin was a Druid, a Celtic priest, and some said he could do magic. His wisdom, understanding, and gentle spirit would help Uther convince the chieftains to join with him and make peace, not war.

One of the first people Uther and Merlin went to see was Gorlois, the lord of Cornwall, in his castle at Tintagel. Gorlois was a good and reasonable man, and he soon agreed to accept Uther's leadership. When their talks were over, Gorlois prepared a huge feast for Uther and his men.

During the feast, Uther looked up, and, across the table, saw the most beautiful woman he had ever laid eyes on.

"Who is that?" Uther asked Merlin.

"That is Igraine, Gorlois's wife," the old man answered.

Uther said nothing, but Merlin saw Uther's eyes gleam just as they did when he was in battle. To Merlin, this could only signal trouble.

Later in the evening, Uther spoke to Merlin again. "I am in love with Igraine!" he whispered. "I must have her for my wife!"

"She is married to Gorlois!" Merlin whispered harshly. "She cannot be yours." But even Merlin knew that it was no use. Once Uther's mind was made up, no one, not even Merlin the Druid, could change it.

Uther left the castle that night, but at daybreak he laid siege to Gorlois's castle in an attempt to steal his lands—and his wife. In the midst of the fighting, Merlin found Uther on his steed, watching the battle from a rocky outcrop.

"What makes you think," Merlin said slowly, "that Igraine will want to marry you after you have killed her husband?"

"I think," replied Uther, smiling, "that she will not know he is dead."

Merlin shook his wise old head. He knew exactly what Uther had in mind, and he knew how determined Uther was.

"I will help you," sighed Merlin, "but only this once. And you must do something for me in return."

"I will do whatever you ask," Uther promised.

"At nightfall," said Merlin, "I will make an enchantment that will turn you into Gorlois. Igraine will welcome you as her husband."

"And what must I do in return?" asked Uther.

"Only this," Merlin replied. "When your son is born, you must give him to me."

Uther turned pale. "You ask a high price for your magic, Merlin," he said.

"Yes," said Merlin, "and you must swear to pay it."

"I swear it," said Uther quietly. "I swear it as your High King."

The battle raged on through the day, neither side gaining the upper hand. As the sun set, Gorlois heard that Uther had retreated.

"We must pursue him!" he cried. He saddled his horse, and rode with twenty of his men out into the darkness.

On the outcrop, Merlin was beginning his enchantment. As he mumbled ancient Celtic spells, a mist began to creep in from the sea. It rose higher and higher, like smoke from a dragon's nose. It encased Uther, and then, as Merlin thrust his staff into a soft patch of earth, it receded and left the two men standing on the outcrop.
But it was no longer Uther who stood before Merlin.
Anyone would have said it was Gorlois.
Anyone, that is, but Merlin.

"Now," said Merlin, helping the new Gorlois onto his horse, "ride!" He slapped the horse on the flank, and it hurtled toward the castle.

Within the castle walls, Morgana, the three-year-old daughter of Gorlois and Igraine, was crying.

"My poor father is dead! My father is dead!" she sobbed.

"No, little one," Igraine crooned, "your father is not dead!" As Igraine stroked her daughter's hair, Gorlois burst through the door.

"See," smiled Igraine, "here is your father now."

"No!" Morgana cried at the man standing before her and her mother. "He is not my father! He is a bad man!" Burying her head in her mother's skirts, she wailed again, "My father is dead! My father is dead!"

Somehow, little Morgana saw something that Igraine could not. Igraine did not know who the man in front of her really was, nor did she know that the real Gorlois, her true husband, lay dead less than a mile away, killed by Uther's men.

Morgana knew, and she cried louder and more bitterly. But all Igraine felt as she sent the sobbing child out of the room was relief and happiness to see her husband alive.

The next morning, Merlin entered the castle at the head of a grim procession carrying Gorlois's body. Using all his powers and his gentle way with words, he managed to explain the events of the previous night to a tearful and distraught Igraine. Somehow he was able to calm and comfort her.

Igraine and Uther were soon married, and Uther took Gorlois's place at Tintagel. Nine months later, in the middle of the bleak British winter, Uther Pendragon's heir was born.

Gazing adoringly at her tiny new son, Igraine rocked the baby tenderly. Suddenly Merlin burst through the door, with Uther behind him.

"Merlin, I beg you to reconsider!" Uther cried.

"You swore by your kingship!" Merlin bellowed. He stormed over to Igraine and, displaying surprising strength for an old man, wrenched the baby from her arms.

"No!" Igraine screamed. "My son!" She could not understand why Merlin had suddenly changed from a kind old man into a vicious thief.

"Please, Merlin, my only son!" begged Uther, trying to stand in the old man's way. "He does not even have a name yet."

With the child still in his arms, Merlin whispered to Uther, "If only you could know what your son will mean to this country." Merlin kissed Uther on both cheeks, then spun around and left, his robes billowing out behind him.

Igraine's screams seared through Uther, his whole body wracked with guilt at the foolish promise he had made.

Later that day, far from Tintagel, Merlin was singing a lullaby to the baby. "Hush, little one," he said when he had finished. "Hush, little Arthur, true king of Britain. You're going to Wales, where you will be safe. Safe, until it is time."

Merlin brought the baby to Ector, a trusted warrior. "Guard him well," he told Ector, "for he is the one."

Uther Pendragon remained High King of Britain for several years, but the guilt of losing his son and breaking his wife's heart was too much for him. He died a shattered man, and, as far as anyone knew, without an heir.

Britain was without a leader once more.

THE SWORD IN THE STONE

The bitter winter wind swirled around Ector and his sons as their horses trudged through the thick snow. The three were making the long journey from their home in the south of Wales to Caerleon for the king-making. The old king was dead, and now the bravest warriors of all the clans in the land were meeting to battle for the right to be Pendragon, High King of Britain.

"Father, I am frozen nearly to death!" moaned Cei, Ector's elder son. "Can we not stop and rest?"

"No!" said Ector. "We are nearly at the battlefield. Look! There are crowds of warriors in front of us!"

"I am too cold and tired to fight!" whined Cei. "I am not meant to be king, so why carry on?"

"I'll not have my son talk in that manner!" bellowed Ector. "Prepare yourself, boy. Take up your sword!"

Cei swung round to reach for his sword. Suddenly he gasped. "Father! My sword is gone!" he said.

"What?" shouted his father. "You cannot become Pendragon without a sword! How could you have been so careless?"

Ector's younger son, Arthur, a boy of only seventeen, spoke up.

"I saw a smithy a few miles back," he said. "I could hurry and fetch Cei a new sword."

Ector broke into a smile. "You see, Cei! Your younger brother has been watchful! Perhaps he would make a better Pendragon! Here is some gold," he said, turning to Arthur. "Go and buy Cei a fine new sword."

Arthur turned his horse and sped off through the snow. But to his dismay, the smithy was shut, and all the doors were barred.

Glancing around, Arthur noticed a path a few yards away. Curious, he followed it into a small grove. In the middle of the grove was a large, moss-covered stone with a sword plunged deep inside it. Nearby lay an old man with long white hair and beard, fast asleep.

"This must be his sword," Arthur thought. "I'm sure he wouldn't mind if I just borrowed it for a while. I'll return it as soon as the battle is over."

Arthur grabbed the weapon and slid it easily from the stone. As he turned to go, he saw his brother riding towards him.

"What's taking you so long, Arthur?" Cei shouted. "The battle is about to start!"

"Sorry, Cei," Arthur stammered. "But look at the magnificent sword I have for you!"

"This is a fine weapon," said Cei, admiring the gleaming blade and the jewel-encrusted handle. "Thank you, Arthur!"

The two rode to the battlefield together. Ector was waiting uneasily, but his impatience turned to amazement when Cei showed him his new sword.

"This is Caliburn, the sword of the Pendragons!" whispered Ector. "This is the prize for the victor in today's battle! Arthur, how did you get it?"

"It was stuck in a stone," Arthur began, "and..." Before he could finish, Cei interrupted.

"...and I pulled it out, Father," said Cei. "Arthur didn't get it, I did. That must make me the Pendragon!"

Hearing Cei's shouts, some of the warriors rode over from the battlefield to see what the commotion was about.

"Show me where you found this, son," said Ector.

The crowd followed Ector and his sons to the grove near the smithy. The old man was awake now, smiling wryly at the group coming toward him.

"Where did you find the sword, Cei?" asked Ector.

Cei looked at the old man, and knew that he couldn't lie any more. "I didn't, Father," he said quietly, hanging his head. "Arthur did."

Stifling his anger, Ector turned to his other son. "Arthur," he said, "show me where you found it."

The crowd held its breath as Arthur put the sword back into the stone.

"What trickery is this?" shouted a man in the crowd. "The sword is meant to be lying on the stone, as a prize for the winner of the battle." More angry shouts joined his.

Holding up his hands for silence, the old man stepped forward.

"This sword is too great a prize for the winner of a mere battle," he said.

"You have come to choose the High King today. A different test is needed. I am Merlin the Druid, and I have put a spell on this sword. Only the one who can draw it from this stone is the true-born King of Britain!"

A great cry arose, and men began pushing forward to get to the sword. But not even the mightiest warrior could budge it. None of these men was the true Pendragon.

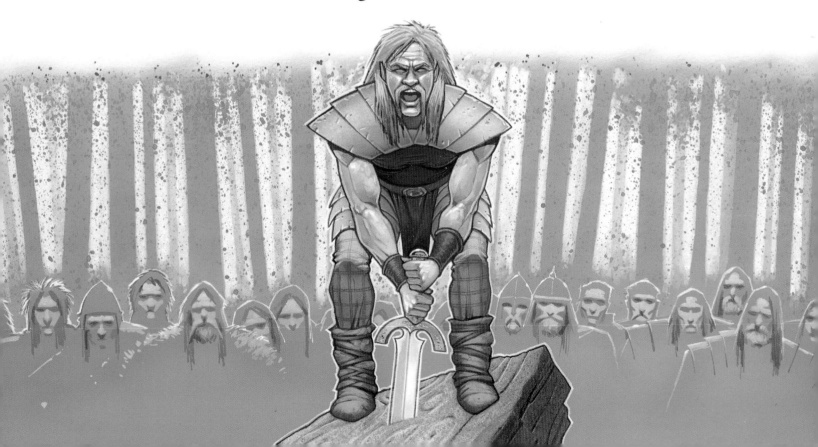

At last only Arthur remained.

"The boy will try now," Ector declared.

"The boy?" someone shouted scornfully. "He's not old enough to shave, much less be Pendragon!" A ripple of laughter ran through the crowd.

"He will try!" said Ector, leading Arthur up to the stone.

Arthur wrapped his hands around the jewel-encrusted handle and pulled. The sword slid from the stone like a fish cutting through the calm waters of a lake.

Instantly, the crowd fell silent.

"How can I be king?" Arthur whispered.

Merlin came forward. "Arthur," he said, "you are the son of Uther Pendragon, clan chieftain and High King of Britain. You are the true Pendragon."

"No!" cried Arthur. "Ector is my father! You are lying, old man!"

"They are not lies, Arthur," said Merlin gently. "I was advisor to your father, and to his father before him. I have been waiting for you."

"Merlin is telling the truth," said Ector, putting his arm around Arthur's trembling shoulders. "He brought you to me when you were only a baby, and told me to raise you as my own. I did not know then who you were. But it is all clear to me now."

"So you are not my father?" Arthur breathed. "Cei is not my brother?"

"I may not be your true father," replied Ector, "but I love you as my own. And because of that love I know that you must take your seat as Pendragon. You are the chosen one, Arthur, whom the Druids of old spoke of in their prophecies. Now your time has come."

Ector kissed Arthur on both cheeks, then stepped back.

"Kneel!" he shouted to the crowd. "Kneel before the Pendragon of Britain!"

Arthur gazed at the sword in his hand. The air was cold, but the sword felt warm and alive, and a surge of energy coursed through Arthur's body.

There, in the winter sun, with the melting snow under his feet, he raised Caliburn above his head. He was no longer just Arthur, a shy and quiet young boy. He was Arthur Pendragon, Chieftain and High King of Britain.

THE SAXON WARS

Britain had a leader at last. But across the sea, her enemies were preparing for war. For years, the Saxons had been waiting to invade Britain. Now that an inexperienced young boy was on the throne, the Saxon king, Aelle, saw his chance. He gathered an army and began invading settlements along Britain's southern coast.

News of the raids reached Arthur, who quickly assembled a war council at Camelot, his fortress in northern Wales. The council was made up of the wisest and bravest chieftains in the land. As they sat at the long table in Camelot's great hall, torches crackling on the walls, a chieftain named Uriens began to laugh.

"What amuses you, Uriens?" Arthur asked.

"You are so young, Arthur," the chieftain replied, "and you know nothing of war. When your father was king, war was a way of life. I was worried at first that it would end under your rule, but now there is the promise of fighting, so my mind is at ease. War stirs the soul, Arthur, and I delight in it!"

For a moment, a biting silence hung in the air. Then Arthur shattered it by slamming his fist down on the table.

"No!" he bellowed. "No councillor of mine shall take delight in the death of others. War is a hateful thing!" He stopped, then spoke again in softer tones. "Nevertheless, if my country requires it, we must fight. We must protect our people and drive the Saxons out."

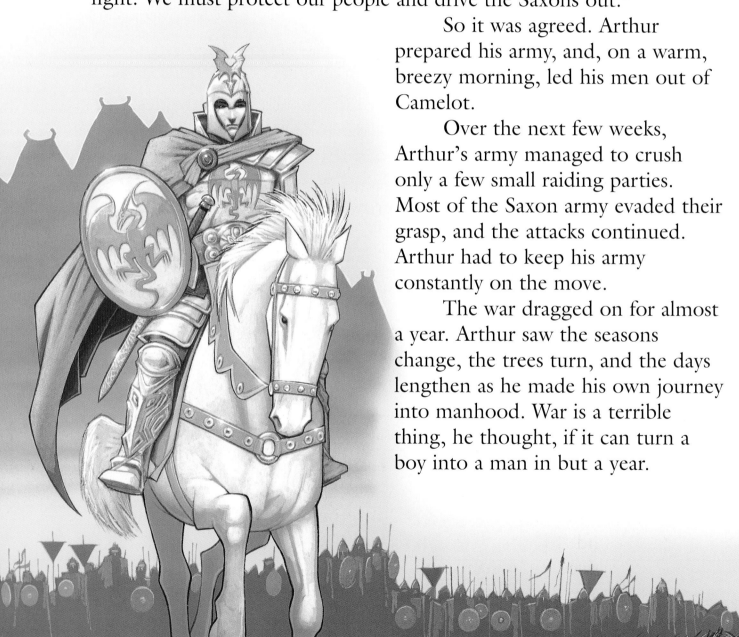

So it was agreed. Arthur prepared his army, and, on a warm, breezy morning, led his men out of Camelot.

Over the next few weeks, Arthur's army managed to crush only a few small raiding parties. Most of the Saxon army evaded their grasp, and the attacks continued. Arthur had to keep his army constantly on the move.

The war dragged on for almost a year. Arthur saw the seasons change, the trees turn, and the days lengthen as he made his own journey into manhood. War is a terrible thing, he thought, if it can turn a boy into a man in but a year.

One night, just after dark, Arthur and his most trusted aides, Cei and Bedwyr, sat around a fire in a grassy field. They talked about military tactics, and about the future and the past. Merlin played his harp and told tales of the bravery of Celtic warriors in days gone by.

Just as they were beginning to grow drowsy, a young messenger galloped up on a tired horse.

"My lord," the boy panted, "the Saxons are taking up positions near Mount Badon. Their entire army has gathered there!"

"Mount Badon?" snapped Bedwyr. "That's just half a day's march from here!"

Mount Badon was a small hill outside Bath, an important city in Roman times. If the Saxons captured the hill, they would be able to take over the city, a perfect place to bring in more men and supplies. But if Arthur and his men defeated the Saxons here, they could drive them out of Britain once and for all. It was the decisive battle they had all been waiting for.

Arthur jumped up and stamped out the fire. "Prepare the men," he told Cei and Bedwyr. "We will march at dawn."

They arrived at Mount Badon just before midday. The Saxons had already begun moving up the hill and so had the advantage of the higher ground. If Arthur charged them now, he would surely lose. The Celts had no choice but to wait for the Saxons to attack.

Arthur rode out in front of his troops. "Many of you will die today," he told them. "I cannot lie about that. What I can say is that in your dying, something far greater will be born—a peaceful, united Britain."

Merlin then said an ancient Druid's blessing over the men, and Arthur arranged the troops to form a shield wall against the Saxon charge. Some mumbled short prayers as they prepared for the attack.

Within seconds, the Saxons began rushing down the hill. Arthur wheeled his steed around and beckoned for a small group of mounted warriors to follow him. As the Saxons reached the shield wall, the Celts on horseback smashed into their flank. The shield wall broke, and the Celts charged the Saxons, scattering them instantly.

But the Saxons managed to recover and retaliate fiercely. The battle raged all day, the clever tactics and passion of Arthur's Celts winning out one minute, the aggression and force of the Saxons taking over the next.

By the time the sun was setting, it was the Celts who had the upper hand. A few stubborn Saxon warriors continued to fight, but most of them willingly surrendered.

The battle was over. The Saxons were defeated. Men lay dead all around, and the soft grass was stained red.

On the crest of Mount Badon, the Saxon king Aelle knelt at Arthur's feet, his hands bound behind his back, Cei's knife at his throat.

"Shall I do it?" Cei asked

"No," Arthur said, drawing Cei's hand away. He untied Aelle and raised him up.

"You fought well. Gather what is left of your army and go home. Do not return here again."

Arthur's aides were as shocked as Aelle, who stared deeply into Arthur's eyes. "You are a worthy opponent, Arthur Pendragon," was all he said.

Arthur Pendragon reassembled his army, raised his banner once more, and began the march back to Camelot. His knights returned to Camelot as the liberators of a nation, and leading them was not a boy, but a man—a man who was a king.

EXCALIBUR

Although Arthur had defeated the Saxon invaders at Mount Badon, a few renegade warriors remained, and in the days following the battle Arthur and his army had several skirmishes with these small Saxon bands.

In one such fight Arthur found himself surrounded by warriors. He whirled his sword around his head like a windmill, and hacked and slashed his way through them. Just as he was stumbling out of the circle they had formed around him, one Saxon brought his sword crashing down on the blade of Arthur's weapon. The metal shattered into several pieces, leaving a useless stump in Arthur's hand.

Arthur rolled to his left to avoid another blow of the weapon, and quickly snatched a sword from a wounded soldier who lay on the ground. He continued fighting with this, and he and his men managed to defeat the Saxons.

After the battle, Arthur returned to the fields where his army had camped, and sought out Merlin.

"Merlin," Arthur said miserably, "look at what the Saxons have done to the sword of the Pendragons."

Merlin said nothing, but took the stump of Arthur's sword from him, and moved silently forward. He motioned for Arthur to mount his horse, and Merlin himself did likewise.

"Where are we going?" the young king asked.

"Follow," was Merlin's only reply. As the late afternoon sun began to sink, he led Arthur down narrow, unfamiliar paths. They rode for what seemed like hours. At last, toward dusk, Merlin alighted and told Arthur to do the same.

Merlin tied both their horses to a pointed rock and beckoned for Arthur to follow him into what looked like a dense forest. It turned out to be nothing more than a thick, circular copse on top of a sloping embankment. Below the embankment was a lake, and on its bank was a stone altar. When he saw it, Arthur knew that he was on sacred ground.

"Look towards the middle of the lake," said Merlin calmly.

Arthur looked out, mesmerized by the magical tranquillity of the surroundings. Suddenly the glassy surface of the lake began to ripple. Arthur bristled with anticipation, then gasped as an arm, clothed all in white, burst through the water. It was holding a sword, which caught the last rays of the sun and reflected them back in a spectacular, fiery display.

The sword was dazzling. Its blade shone with the radiance of the brightest star, and its jewel-encrusted handle and hilt were engraved with intricate carvings.

"Take it!" whispered Merlin. "Take the sword! It's yours."

"But how shall I get it?" whispered Arthur.

Merlin jabbed a finger towards the water's edge, where Arthur saw a small boat bobbing gently near the shore. Arthur was certain it hadn't been there when they arrived.

"What...?" he breathed.

"Get in!" ordered Merlin.

Arthur did so, and Merlin stepped in after him.

Merlin pointed his staff, and the boat began to slice its way through the water towards the arm. When they reached it, Arthur stretched out a hand and took the sword. He held it up and admired its immense beauty.

"It is your sword, Arthur," said Merlin. "It is Excalibur, forged in Avalon, the Otherworld, by the Lady of the Lake herself."

Arthur was awestruck. The Lady of the Lake—the powerful spirit who guarded the entrance to the Otherworld—had blessed him with this sword! All the way back to shore, he gazed at it, too overcome to speak, or even to read the words he saw engraved on the blade.

When they were back on land, Merlin drew a golden scabbard from within the folds of his robe and held it out to Arthur.

"This is the scabbard for your sword," he explained.

Arthur was disappointed. Next to the splendid sword, the scabbard looked plain and unimportant.

"Which do you like more," Merlin asked, "the sword or the scabbard?"

Arthur could not lie. "The sword," he replied. "I can win wars and defend my land and people with this magnificent sword. But what use is the scabbard to me, especially one so ordinary? I could easily do without it."

"Looks can be deceiving," Merlin said. "The sword will serve you well, but with this scabbard at your side, no sword, spear, nor any weapon carried by any son of earth shall harm you. Take good care of the sword, Arthur, but make certain you never lose the scabbard."

That night, before he lay down to rest, Arthur took a final look at his new sword. This time, he looked closely at the words etched on the blade.

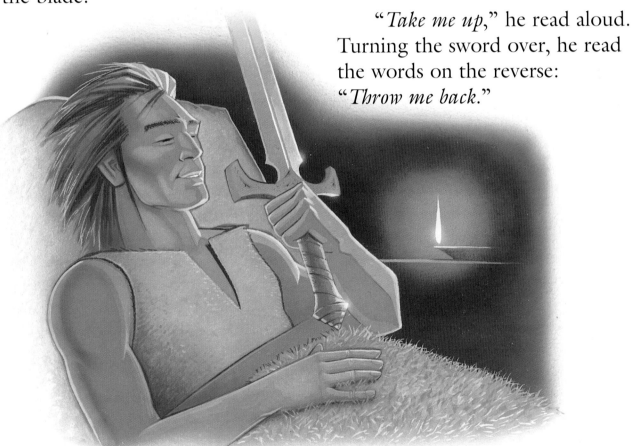

"*Take me up,*" he read aloud. Turning the sword over, he read the words on the reverse: "*Throw me back.*"

The words were as mysterious to Arthur as everything else that had happened that day. With a yawn, he replaced the sword in the scabbard and, clutching it to him to keep it safe, he was soon fast asleep. When he awoke the next morning, he once again gazed in wonder at the beauty of this mighty sword … his sword: Excalibur.

THE BIRTH
OF A DREAM

The responsibility of being king weighed heavily on Arthur. After Mount Badon, he spent more and more time alone, thinking and worrying. He still joined his warriors for games and battle practice, but in the evenings he disappeared to dine alone in his room. Merlin tried to coax him back, saying that the men missed him. But Arthur kept to his solitary ways, joining the others only when there was a visiting chieftain. Arthur did not enjoy these formal meetings, but he knew that they were necessary to keep the tribal leaders loyal.

One of those leaders was Leodegrance, an old friend of Uther, Arthur's father. A few months after Mount Badon, Leodegrance came to feast with Arthur. He and his procession arrived early in the morning, and Arthur spent the day showing the chieftain around Camelot and introducing him to some of his warriors. Leodegrance seemed impressed.

When darkness fell, Arthur, Merlin, and Arthur's closest warriors piled into the great hall, followed by Leodegrance and his aides. But Leodegrance would not sit down.

"Where is Guinevere?" he shouted, looking toward the door. Suddenly a smile spread across his face.

"My dear!" he said, opening his arms to the young woman who was just entering.

Arthur turned to look, and what he saw took his breath away.

She is beauty itself, Arthur thought, gazing at the vision who was walking toward Leodegrance. Her flame-red hair cascaded down her back like a gentle summer rainfall, and her hazel eyes were lit by a soft, warm smile.

Arthur was enchanted. But he knew that his father had been captivated by another man's wife in just this way, so he chose his words carefully.

"Your wife is truly beautiful, Leodegrance," Arthur said.

Leodegrance roared with laughter. "Would that I had a wife so young or so beautiful!" he said. "Guinevere is my daughter!"

Arthur breathed a sigh of relief. "Forgive me," he said sheepishly.

Throughout the feast, Leodegrance chatted to Arthur, but Arthur was not really listening. He spent the whole evening gazing at Guinevere. The next morning, he went to speak to Merlin.

"You know, Merlin," he began, "I have been lonely recently. I am a king … and a king should have a queen."

Merlin sighed. "You'll have to ask Leodegrance first," he said.

Arthur grinned shyly. "How did you know?" he asked.

"The simplest of fools would know, Arthur," Merlin replied.

Later that morning, Arthur invited Leodegrance to stay for another week.

Leodegrance smiled knowingly. "Arthur," he said, "you have my permission and my blessing to court my daughter. We will stay six more days."

Arthur shook his head, realizing how obvious his wishes were. But he was pleased.

Over the next few days, Arthur and Guinevere spent a great deal of time together. They went for walks and rides, and stayed up talking late into the night. When it was time for Guinevere and her father to leave, Arthur went with them to the gate.

"Guinevere," he said, "I have felt lonely until now, bearing the burden of a kingdom on my shoulders. But when I am with you, I feel whole. Will you be my queen?"

Guinevere smiled. Over the past few days, she too had fallen in love, and she had been waiting and hoping for this moment.

"Yes," she replied.

A month later, Leodegrance and Guinevere returned to Camelot, along with loyal chieftains from across the land who had come to pay homage to the Pendragon on his wedding day.

Merlin conducted the ceremony. Once it was over, and before the festivities began, Arthur and Guinevere were led into the great hall. There, in place of the old long, narrow table, they saw a round one, majestic and gleaming in the torchlight.

"The Round Table," said Leodegrance, "is my wedding present to you and your queen, Pendragon."

As Arthur thanked Leodegrance, a vision began forming in his mind: he saw all the chieftains of all the clans of Britain gathered around one table, discussing laws and debating issues together, keeping the peace of the land. With this table as his symbol, he could unite the island.

He asked all the chieftains present to sit down at the table. Then he stood to address them.

"My lords," he said, "we have fought together against the Saxons. War creates a bond between men, and tonight we must strengthen that bond, so that it never breaks. Here, at this table, we are all equal. The Round Table has no head, nor any foot. Although we hail from different tribes and clans, at the Round Table we are all Celts of Britain, with an equal voice."

Some warriors banged their fists on the table in approval, and cries of "Hear! Hear!" echoed around the room.

"We will meet here twice in every month," Arthur continued. "As we are united around this table, so shall we be united Celts in Britain!"

The chieftains clapped and cheered. There, in the great hall of Camelot, on the night of Arthur Pendragon's wedding to Guinevere, the dream of the Round Table was born.

GAWAIN AND THE GREEN KNIGHT

It was midwinter, and bitter cold. In the great hall of Camelot the knights of the Round Table sat wrapped in their cloaks, eagerly awaiting the meal that would soon come steaming from the great hearth in the next room.

To pass the time before the food arrived, King Arthur proposed that a tale should be told, one of bravery and great deeds. Arthur turned to Merlin, but before the old man had a chance to rise, there was a thunderous clattering at the gates, and a rider burst through the doors.

The men were taken aback. No one entered the hall of Camelot on horseback, let alone unannounced and without permission. When they took a closer look at their guest, they had an even bigger surprise.

Everything about the man—his skin, his clothes, his horse, his hair—was green. Only the whites of his eyes and his gleaming white teeth

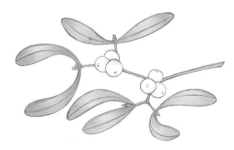

shone through the mask of green. In one hand he carried a large axe. In the other he held a sprig of mistletoe, a holy plant to the Celts, to show that he did not come in anger.

"Men of Camelot, I come in friendship," said the Green Knight, getting down from his horse and laying his axe on the floor. "To entertain you on this coldest of all nights, I present you with a challenge: I ask that one man here come forward, and, with one blow, strike off my head with this weapon."

There was a small murmur from the men, but it was quickly hushed as the Green Knight spoke again. "There is just one condition," he added. "I am to do the same to him in a year and a day."

The hall was silent. Not a single warrior wished to take up the terrifying Green Knight's challenge.

The Green Knight began to laugh—so loudly that the walls shook. "I had heard," he roared, "that the men of the Round Table were the bravest in all the land. Now I see the truth, and I am quite disappointed."

This was too much for Arthur. He could not have his loyal, courageous warriors spoken of this way. He stood up.

"I will do it, sir," he announced to the Green Knight.

But before Arthur could step forward, Gawain, a young warrior from the far north, stopped him.

"No. The Pendragon must not go," said Gawain. "I will do it." He turned to address the Green Knight. "I am Gawain. I accept your challenge."

"Gawain, you are a credit to yourself and this table," said the Green Knight. "Come and take my axe."

Gawain did so, and the Green Knight knelt and bared his neck.

"One blow, Gawain," he reminded him.

Gawain struggled to lift the heavy axe, but at last he held it over his head and took his swing. He made a clean cut through the Green Knight's neck. Instantly his head fell from his body and rolled across the floor.

Gawain jumped back. But instead of toppling over, the Green Knight got up, walked over to his head, and picked it up by the hair.

The head cleared its throat and fixed its eyes on Gawain. Then it spoke.

"You will find me at the Green Tower," it said, "in a year and a day."

With his head under his arm, the Green Knight picked up his axe, hopped onto his horse, and galloped out as quickly as he had arrived, leaving the men in the hall stunned.

The year passed quickly. Everyone seemed to forget the Green Knight's challenge— everyone but Gawain. He worried about it all year, and when the time finally came for him to leave, he was filled with dread.

"Good luck, Gawain. Return safely," Arthur said as he watched him go. In his heart, though, Arthur did not believe he would ever see Gawain again.

Gawain rode for days through treacherous, frozen woodland paths. Bands of robbers roamed the forests, and wild beasts howled all around him. Gawain took shelter in peasants' cottages and woodcutters' huts, and wherever he went he asked the way to the Green Tower. Still, he was never sure he was going in the right direction.

Finally, just a few days before he was supposed to meet the Green Knight, Gawain was close to giving up. Icy sleet lashed down from the sky, and he felt he did not have the strength to go on. But just as he was about to turn back to Camelot, he saw a fortress on the horizon, and galloped toward it. When he arrived he banged hard on the gate, and begged the gatekeeper to let him in.

The lord of the fortress came to meet Gawain in the courtyard.

"I am Bertilak," he said. "We are privileged to welcome a knight of the Round Table."

After dinner that evening, Bertilak invited Gawain to stay for a few days. When Gawain explained that he had to be at the Green Tower in four days, Bertilak exclaimed, "The Green Tower is less than a day's ride from here! Stay for another three days."

Then Bertilak suggested that they play a game over the next few days. "Anything that I acquire while you're here I'll give to you, and you must do the same for me."

The game seemed a little strange to Gawain, but he agreed.

Early the next morning, Gawain was awakened by a knock at the door. It was Bertilak's beautiful wife, who came in and sat on the bed.

"Good morning, Gawain," she said. "I have heard many tales of your bravery in the wars. Such courage deserves a reward."

She leaned toward Gawain and kissed him.

Stunned, Gawain could only murmur, "Thank you, my lady."

The lady just smiled and left.

That afternoon, when Bertilak returned from the hunt, he presented Gawain with a small fox.

"And what do you have for me?" he asked.

In reply, Gawain reached up and kissed Bertilak, who roared with laughter.

"I won't ask how you came by that!" he chuckled.

The next morning the lady visited Gawain again, and again she kissed him. Later, Bertilak again presented Gawain with the morning's catch, and again received a kiss.

"You're a lucky man to be getting all these kisses," he laughed.

On the third day, the lady came to Gawain yet again.

"You go to meet the Green Knight tomorrow. Please take this," she said, holding out a green sash. "If you wear it, nothing will harm you."

Then, as before, she kissed him and left.

When Bertilak returned, the usual exchange took place—he gave Gawain a squirrel, and Gawain gave him a kiss. But Gawain did not give Bertilak the sash, knowing that without it he would surely die.

The next morning, Gawain wrapped the sash around his waist and followed Bertilak's directions to the Green Tower. The Green Knight was waiting for him, axe in hand.

"I am pleased to see you have kept your promise," boomed the huge man. "Now, kneel."

Gawain did so, and clenched his fists, waiting for the blow. He felt the air rush across his neck as the Green Knight's axe came down. But the blade never struck him.

"What trickery is this?" he shouted.

"I am allowed one blow," the Green Knight replied. "That was not a blow."

He raised the weapon again, but again he stopped before he hit Gawain's neck. Then he raised the axe a third time and brought it down. This time it just scraped Gawain's neck. Jumping up, Gawain drew his sword.

"You have had your blow!" he cried. "Now prepare to fight!"

"Put away your sword, Gawain," the Green Knight said calmly. "You are in no danger from me."

"Why?" asked Gawain. "Who are you?"

"I am Bertilak," he replied, "the very man you have been staying with for the past three days."

"B-but…," stammered Gawain, "how can that be?"

"Morgana, half-sister of Arthur Pendragon, placed me under a spell," said Bertilak, "and turned me into the Green Knight. She sent me to test the bravery of Camelot's warriors, and so I offered my challenge—the challenge only you were bold enough to accept."

"But why did you not cut off my head?" asked Gawain.

"I missed you the first two times because you kept your promise to me and gave me the kisses I had told my wife to give you. I scratched you the third time because although you gave the kiss, you kept the sash."

Gawain looked down, ashamed. "I have been dishonest," he admitted. "I don't deserve my seat at the Round Table, and I didn't deserve your hospitality." He knelt again. "Take my head."

"Get up, Gawain," said Bertilak. "Nobody is perfect, but you have come closer than most. Go back to Camelot with pride—you are an almost perfect knight."

Everyone at Camelot was astonished when Gawain returned, alive and well. When he told his amazing tale, Arthur decreed that every year, on the anniversary of his return, everyone at the Round Table should wear a green sash to remember the deeds of Gawain, the almost perfect knight.

LANCELOT

Just before dawn, a small ship drifted to shore on the rocky Welsh coast. A moment later, its two passengers alighted onto the wet sand, followed by their horses, prompted down the gangplank by the crew. Then, lest they be mistaken for Saxon raiders, the crew heaved the boat back into the tide and began rowing home to Brittany.

The two men who stood on the beach were dressed in simple tunics and plaid trousers. At the side of the taller of the two men hung a short sword.

"Come," he said, as they mounted their horses, "let us find the king."

Later that morning, rain splashed down on the fortress of Camelot. Inside the castle walls, Arthur and Cei were saddling their horses.

"Must we go riding?" grumbled Cei. "Look at the weather."

"It's just rain," Arthur replied. "It won't hurt us."

Cei sighed. Arthur might have been his younger foster brother, but he was also the king—and he had a mind of his own, which could not often be changed. When Arthur jumped on his horse and galloped off, Cei reluctantly followed.

In a field barely half a mile away, two riders had tied their horses to a gnarled old oak tree, and were sheltering beneath the broad branches.

Suddenly Arthur and Cei rode into the field. The men under the tree had no idea who they were, but the taller one said something to his companion. Then he mounted his horse and cantered over, blocking Arthur's way.

"Please move aside, sir," said Arthur.

"Fight me first," was the reply.

Arthur was taken aback. "Why do you seek a fight?" he asked.

"I merely seek my match," the man replied. "In all my years, I have never been beaten. I came here looking for someone worthy of my service. Perhaps King Arthur himself will ride by and accept my challenge."

Deciding not to reveal his identity yet, Arthur peered into the stranger's eyes. They fixed him with their gaze, so that although Arthur knew he should refuse, he could not say the words. Instead, he turned his horse around and prepared to charge.

"What are you doing?" roared Cei. "What if you lose?"

Arthur was asking himself the same thing—but he had no answer. He just drew his sword and galloped toward his challenger, leaning over to swing at him. The stranger deftly ducked out of the way, then spun around in the saddle and struck Arthur on the back with the hilt of his sword. Arthur was thrown to the ground, and Excalibur went flying.

As the stranger dismounted, Arthur rolled over and grabbed Excalibur. Springing to his feet, he thrust the sword at his opponent. The blow was deflected, and Arthur made another attempt. This too was parried, but Arthur would not give up. Eventually, he forced his opponent back to the tree in the middle of the field, and it looked as if he had won the fight. But as he drew his arm back for the final swing, the challenger vaulted out of the way, so that Arthur's sword was plunged into the tree trunk.

Cei spurred his horse across the field. "Arthur!" he cried, moving in front of Arthur to protect him. But the challenger was not attacking. He was staring at the two men.

"Arthur?" whispered the
young man. "*King* Arthur?"

Arthur looked at the
ground. "Yes," he said at last.
"I am the Pendragon."

The stranger continued to
stare. The man before him was a
sorry sight. His face was bleeding,
his hair was matted, and his
clothes were caked with mud.

"I don't believe you," the
stranger declared.

"Very well," said Arthur. He
pulled Excalibur from the tree
trunk and held it out. The man
gazed at the ornately decorated
handle and the carvings on the
blade, then fell to his knees.

"Your Majesty," he said, clasping Arthur's hand, "I am Lancelot,
son of King Ban of Brittany. The true reason I came here was to seek a
place at your Round Table, a place at your right hand!"

Arthur looked down at the young man. His intuition told him
that anyone with such boldness, skill, and strength was more than
worthy of a place at the Round Table. But as a wise king, he knew how
reckless it would be to grant a total stranger a place at the Table
without first testing him.

"Come," said Arthur, beckoning the man to rise. "Return with us
to Camelot, and we will talk."

Over the days that followed, Lancelot went everywhere with Arthur.
He told him about his upbringing in Brittany and how, as a boy, he had
begun training to become the greatest warrior the world had ever seen.

"Although I am not a native of Britain," he told Arthur, "when I
heard about the Round Table, and your dream of unity, I had only one
wish—to join, and become part of something truly noble."

Lancelot had been at Camelot for two weeks when word came that the fortress of one of Arthur's loyal chieftains was under siege by a band of rebel clansmen.

Lancelot begged Arthur to let him free the castle. Arthur consented, asking Bedwyr to accompany him, along with a small band of warriors.

A week later, the men returned, victorious.

"I've never seen anything like it," Bedwyr told Arthur. "As a leader, he is incredible. And he fights like one possessed. He won the battle almost single-handedly."

Arthur turned to Lancelot. "My kingdom is in your debt," he said. "How can I repay you?"

"Milord," Lancelot replied, "you know my only wish."

At the next meeting of the Round Table, when all the chieftains of Britain were gathered in Camelot's hall, a new warrior took his place among them. He was brave, noble, virtuous, and believed with his whole heart in the dream of unity.

His name was Lancelot, and he sat at the right hand of King Arthur.

LANCELOT'S TREACHERY

Lancelot had been in Britain for about a year now, and he was never far from Arthur's side. To Arthur, he was a close and trusted friend—but Arthur's warriors and chieftains felt threatened by Lancelot. They resented him, because his virtue and loyalty pointed up their own faults and weaknesses.

Unlike most of the other chieftains and warriors at the table, Lancelot lived at Camelot. Since he was not from Britain, he had no tribe or clan of his own, and no fortress. He was close to the king all the time, and so was always the first to know Arthur's plans.

"When the Round Table began it was a symbol of unity and fairness. No one man was better than another," Cei reminded Arthur. "But you go to Lancelot before any of your other warriors. We might as well not have the meetings of the Table!"

"Don't be ridiculous, Cei," Arthur snapped. But deep down he knew that Cei was right.

Arthur decided that he needed to find somewhere for Lancelot to live, away from Camelot—and he had his own reason for this, different from that of his men.

Arthur had noticed that his queen, Guinevere, had been spending more and more time with Lancelot recently. At first, she too had disliked his arrogance, but her feelings changed as she got to know him better. When Arthur mentioned this to her, she insisted that they were just friends. But both she and Arthur knew that wasn't true. The friendship had deepened into love.

Now Arthur felt that he was trapped in a nightmare, caught between the two people he cared most about: his wife and his best friend. He didn't want to lose either of them. For the time being, finding Lancelot a place to live was all he could do.

Two weeks earlier, the chieftain of the fortress that Lancelot had freed had died. He left no son, and Arthur saw a chance to give Lancelot a home and an adopted clan. The clanspeople did not object—they still saw Lancelot as their rescuer, and were glad to welcome him as their chieftain.

But Arthur could not keep Lancelot away from Camelot all the time. He still returned for meetings of the Round Table, giving him opportunities to meet secretly with Guinevere.

One such night, after the meeting of the Round Table had ended, Guinevere and Lancelot were alone in a half-forgotten, empty room. They were deep in conversation when Lancelot suddenly fell silent. There were voices outside. Slowly, Lancelot crept toward the door, but before he reached it six men burst into the room.

"Treachery!" one screamed. "Lancelot is a traitor!"

The men were fully armed, and Lancelot had nothing but a small dagger. He ran to protect Guinevere as the men attacked. When he could no longer fend them off, he grabbed Guinevere by the hand and bolted for the door.

They sped through the fortress, the shouts of their pursuers behind them. The men caught up to the fleeing pair just in time to see them mount two horses and hurtle out of Camelot into the blackness.

The next day, after Arthur had been told what had happened, the Round Table sat for another meeting.

"What were you doing outside that room?" the king asked the six men.

"We were just passing by," one of them replied.

"You were just passing by," Arthur repeated. "You just happened to be passing a room that no one uses, and all six of you happened to be together, fully armed? You are lying! Get out!" he roared. Then he buried his face in his hands.

When he looked up, he saw that only five of the men had left. One remained, hovering above Lancelot's empty seat.

"Forgive me, milord," he said, "but, liars or not, we have nonetheless shown Lancelot—and, with respect, the queen—to be traitors. They should be dealt with as any other traitors."

Arthur looked up at the man. He had sickly pale skin and a scrawny frame. His greasy black hair flopped across his face, and his sunken, shadowed eyes made him look far older than he probably was. Arthur did not recognize him.

"Who are you?" he asked.

"My name is Mordred, sire," the young man answered. "I am the son of Morgana and Lot, lord of the Orkneys. I am your nephew."

Arthur had not known that he had a nephew, and right now he was too upset to care.

"Leave me, Mordred," he ordered.

"But he is right!" a chieftain shouted from across the table. "Lancelot has probably returned to Brittany, and he has your queen with him! This calls for war!"

Arthur could not find the words to express how deeply he did not want to wage war on Lancelot. He had seen too much bloodshed in his reign already.

It was Cei who put into words what Arthur—and everyone else at the table—was thinking.

"Brother," Cei said gently, "you have no choice."

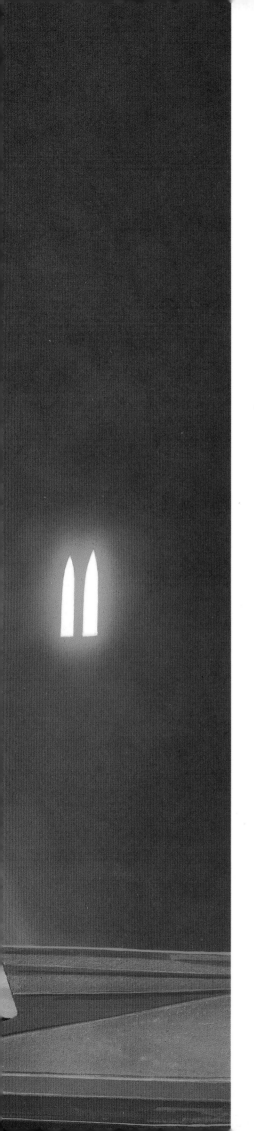

MORGANA AND MORDRED

In the great hall of Camelot, Mordred laughed wickedly. His laughter echoed around the empty hall, flew through the gates of Camelot, and made its way to Brittany, where King Arthur and his army were camped in a field outside Lancelot's castle.

Arthur had just received the news that Mordred had taken his throne, claiming the title of Pendragon. Arthur's nightmare was spinning out of control. If he went back to Britain he would lose both Lancelot and Guinevere forever. If he stayed here, all his work—and his hopes and dreams—would be lost along with his crown.

For an agonized day and night, Arthur stayed in his tent alone, thinking. Merlin wasn't with him—but Arthur tried to remember all the advice his wise teacher had ever given him. At last, just after sunrise, Arthur called Gawain and Bedwyr to his tent. "Take a message to Lancelot and Guinevere," he said. "Tell them to meet me at sunset, in the forest half a mile south."

Sunset came, and Arthur waited in the wooded glade. The leaves cut up the last rays of the sun, casting a lacy pattern on the forest floor. For a few minutes, Arthur forgot his problems and let himself slip into oneness with the forest.

The cracking of a twig disturbed his thoughts. He looked up and saw two figures walking toward him.

Lancelot approached Arthur first. Falling to his knees, he clasped Arthur's hand to his face.

"Forgive me," he wept.

Arthur raised him up, and Lancelot stepped aside, his eyes cast down. Guinevere, her face shining with tears, rushed forward into Arthur's arms.

"What will become of us?" she sobbed.

Gently, Arthur led her over to Lancelot.

"Mordred, my nephew, has usurped my kingdom," Arthur told them. "I would sooner die than see Britain fall into the wrong hands. I must return and fight for what I believe in, for what I have spent my life building. Go back to your castle, Lancelot, and take my queen with you." He gripped Lancelot's hand, held it tightly, then turned to leave.

"Arthur, no!" cried Guinevere, running after him. "I want to go back with you!"

"Guinevere," Arthur said, wiping a tear from her cheek, "when my country has needed me, I have always had to be a king before a husband. That is truer now than ever, though it breaks my heart. Goodbye, my love."

When Arthur was born, his mother, Igraine, already had a daughter, Morgana. Her father was Gorlois, Igraine's first husband. Morgana grew up knowing that her father had been tricked and killed by Arthur's father, Uther Pendragon. The knowledge made her angry and bitter, and by the age of fifteen she had sworn revenge upon her brother, the last remnant of Uther's foul dishonesty.

Morgana trained as a priestess in the Celtic religion, and, with time, developed powers to rival those of Merlin himself. At a young age she had married Lot, chieftain of the Orkney Isles. Within a year they had a son and named him Mordred.

As she sat by the fire, rocking her baby, Morgana crooned to him:

"Mordred, Mordred, my sweet child, you are the one. You are the one to defeat my brother, and lay to rest the evil from which he sprang."

Now Mordred was a young man. He had been well taught, both in the arts of war and the craft of magic. But he had no wish to use his powers and skills for good purposes. His mother had filled him with hatred for Arthur, and all he wanted was to destroy Arthur's dreams and ideals.

As soon as Arthur left for Brittany, Mordred began creating conflict among the clans Arthur had worked so hard to unite. He sent false messages to the chieftains, telling them that another chieftain wanted their land, or that Arthur was taking away their place at the Round Table. Soon the chieftains had turned against one another, and against Arthur. When Mordred offered them a chance of revenge by joining his growing army, they accepted eagerly.

Once he had most of the chieftains on his side, Mordred sent messengers across the sea to Cerdic, a Saxon king who had supported the invasion of Britain years earlier.

"Arthur is weakened," the messengers reported. "Mordred, the successor and next Pendragon, offers you the chance to share the rule with him if you help him end Arthur's reign."

Cerdic was delighted, and gathered his army at once.

Now Arthur had little hope. His army, though brave and experienced, was tiny. He had only a handful of troops and the few chieftains he had taken with him to Brittany. When they returned home and landed on the south coast of Britain, they received word that Mordred and Cerdic's army was already marching toward Camlann, in Cornwall.

"We can't fight them!" the chieftains told Arthur. "We're vastly outnumbered!"

"Yes, that is true," Arthur agreed. "But what if we don't fight? Then I surrender my crown, Mordred becomes Pendragon, and he'll probably have us slaughtered anyway. If we fight," Arthur went on, "then at least we have the chance to defend what we have all worked so hard to achieve. If the dream of the Round Table must die, it should die with honour."

Arthur's words stirred within his men the same courage and passion they had felt at Mount Badon. They were ready to fight and die for their country once more.

THE FINAL BATTLE

In his tent in a field near Camlann, King Arthur warmed himself by a small fire. Excalibur lay across his lap. It was dull, and scratched and chipped from the many battles it had seen. I have spent too much of my reign at war, he thought sadly.

"My lord," said Bedwyr, interrupting his thoughts, "your only choice is to meet Mordred in battle."

Arthur sighed. "Mordred is my own flesh and blood, but I fear you are right. I must speak to the men."

Riding out to the head of his army, Arthur knew that it was outnumbered by the hordes led by Cerdic and Mordred. But Arthur had something his enemies didn't. His men believed with all their hearts in the dream of Britain, and they were willing to die for it.

"Men of Britain," Arthur shouted, "today, you are not fighting for me or even for my kingdom, but for your children's future and the future of your homeland. You are fighting for our dream. Do not let it die."

For a second or two, silence hung in the air. Then a colossal cheer rose from the men. Arthur drew Excalibur and held it aloft. "Forward!" he cried.

But even the Celts' passion could not overcome the sheer numbers of Mordred and Cerdic's army. They suffered heavy losses, and Arthur was forced to retreat.

The Saxons cheered when they saw the Celts falling back. But across the field, Arthur was rallying his troops again.

"We have but one chance," Arthur told his men. "We must make them charge us, then attack their flank with our cavalry. It worked at Mount Badon. We can only pray it will save us now."

The army formed a shield wall, and just as Arthur predicted, the Saxons charged, allowing Arthur to lead his small cavalry force into the flank of Mordred's army. The cavalry's assault sent the Saxons into confusion, leaving them open to attack by the shield wall.

Soon the Celts had cut a swathe of destruction through the enemy troops. Saxons lay dead all around, but for every Saxon that fell, six more seemed to spring up. One man grappled at Arthur's side, tearing his scabbard from his belt. Remembering Merlin's prophecy, Arthur tried to retrieve it, but it was lost in the turmoil of battle.

Despite their gains, the Celts could not take the lead. Yet they fought on. By sunset, both sides had suffered enormous losses.

Earlier, Arthur had seen Cerdic fleeing the field, but there had been no sign of Mordred. Now, on the horizon, Arthur saw his nephew's silhouetted figure, mounted on a horse.

The time has come, Arthur told himself, and rode toward him.

Mordred turned and galloped to meet him. As they collided, Arthur swung Excalibur and sent Mordred flying from his saddle. But Mordred leaped up, and pierced the flank of Arthur's horse. Arthur tumbled down, but, still holding on to his sword, he got to his feet and grabbed Mordred. Before he could deliver his final blow, Mordred thrust his spear into Arthur's stomach.

A searing pain twisted through Arthur's body. Summoning his last ounce of strength, he raised Excalibur and brought it down on Mordred's skull. Instantly, the young man fell dead.

Arthur stumbled backwards. He tried to remove the spear from his body, but the pain was too great, and he collapsed, mortally wounded.

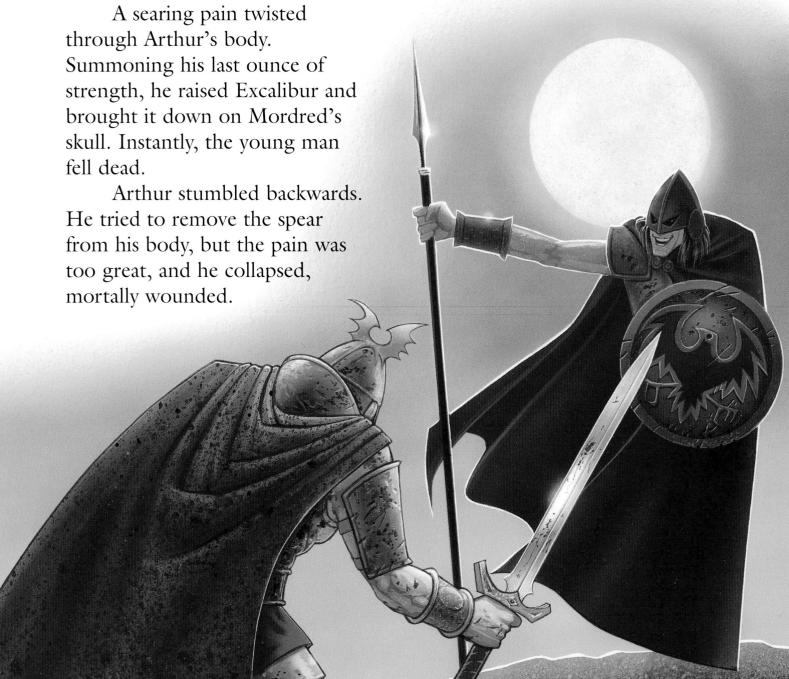

After what seemed like an age, Arthur felt a hand on his forehead. It was Bedwyr. Arthur could see that he had been crying.

"What happened?" Arthur gasped. "What of the dream?"

"The dream is dead, my lord," replied Bedwyr.

Arthur sighed. "Take my sword," he whispered, "and ride north with it. You will find a holy grove, where the Druids used to pray, and a pool. Cast Excalibur into it."

Bedwyr found the place after only a short ride. It was a Celtic custom to throw objects into water as offerings to the gods, but Bedwyr thought of what Excalibur stood for, and could not let it go. Then he noticed the engraving on the blade.

Take me up, it said.

He could not cast it away.

When Bedwyr returned, Arthur asked him, "What did you see when you threw in the sword?"

"Just the wind on the water," Bedwyr answered.

"You are lying," Arthur said. "Go back and do as I have asked."

Wondering how Arthur could have known, Bedwyr went back to the pool. But he still could not let the sword go.

"I couldn't do it, my lord," he told Arthur when he returned, "not when I read the message on the blade!"

"Turn it over, " Arthur told him, "and read the other side."

"*Throw me back*," Bedwyr read aloud.

"When the time is right," Arthur said, "a king will come, and Excalibur will return. The dream will be born again. Until then, you must do as your king commands you. Just this last time, old friend."

With Arthur's words ringing in his head, Bedwyr galloped back to the pool. This time he flung Excalibur in without hesitating. A white-sleeved arm rose from the water. It caught the sword and drew it under the surface.

Bedwyr sped back to tell Arthur what he had seen, but found only some flattened reeds where the king had been lying. In the distance, he saw a black barge sailing through the mist toward the sea. He knew that it was taking Arthur Pendragon, the greatest of all kings, to his final home.

EPILOGUE

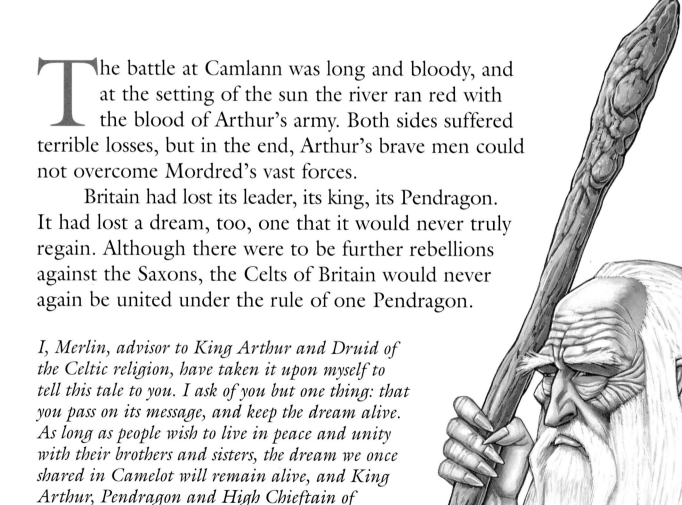

The battle at Camlann was long and bloody, and at the setting of the sun the river ran red with the blood of Arthur's army. Both sides suffered terrible losses, but in the end, Arthur's brave men could not overcome Mordred's vast forces.

Britain had lost its leader, its king, its Pendragon. It had lost a dream, too, one that it would never truly regain. Although there were to be further rebellions against the Saxons, the Celts of Britain would never again be united under the rule of one Pendragon.

I, Merlin, advisor to King Arthur and Druid of the Celtic religion, have taken it upon myself to tell this tale to you. I ask of you but one thing: that you pass on its message, and keep the dream alive. As long as people wish to live in peace and unity with their brothers and sisters, the dream we once shared in Camelot will remain alive, and King Arthur, Pendragon and High Chieftain of Britain, will never die.